COSMIC BLACKOUT!

By Ray O'Ryan

Illustrated by Jason Kraft

LITTLE SIMON
New York London Toronto Sydney New Delhi

LITTLE SIMON
An imprint of Simon & Schuster Children's Publishing Division
1230 Avenue of the Americas, New York, New York 10020
First Little Simon paperback edition November 2017

Also available in a Little Simon hardcover edition.

For information about special discounts for bulk purchases, please contact Simon & Schuster Special Sales at 1-866-506-1949 or business@simonandschuster.com.
The Simon & Schuster Speakers Bureau can bring authors to your live event. For more information or to book an event contact the Simon & Schuster Speakers Bureau at 1-866-248-3049 or visit our website at www.simonspeakers.com.
Designed by Nick Sciacca
Manufactured in the United States of America 1017 MTN
1 2 3 4 5 6 7 8 9 10
Library of Congress Cataloging-in-Publication Data
Names: O'Ryan, Ray, author. | Kraft, Jason (Jason E.), illustrator.
Title: Cosmic blackout! / by Ray O'Ryan ; illustrated by Jason Kraft.
Description: First Little Simon paperback edition. | New York : Little Simon, 2017. | Series: Galaxy Zack ; #16 | Summary: Zack loves everything about his new planet, Nebulon, until there is a complete cosmic blackout and he must try to function without his Indoor Robotic Assistant and hyperphone.
Identifiers: LCCN 2017016642 | ISBN 9781481499897 (pbk) | ISBN 9781481499903 (hc) ISBN 9781481499910 (eBook)
Subjects: | CYAC: Electric power failures—Fiction. | Science fiction. | BISAC: JUVENILE FICTION / Science Fiction. | JUVENILE FICTION / Action & Adventure / General. | JUVENILE FICTION / Readers / Chapter Books.
Classification: LCC PZ7.O7843 Cos 2017 | DDC [Fic]—dc23
LC record available at https://lccn.loc.gov/2017016642K

CONTENTS

Chapter 1
A Strange Dinner

Zack Nelson jumped into the elevator. It was dinnertime on Nebulon, but he was hungry for his favorite breakfast—cosmic cakes with boingoberry syrup. Ira, the Nelson family's Indoor Robotic Assistant, made it for Zack almost every day.

The elevator doors opened and Zack's twin sisters stepped inside.

"I want a galactic patty . . ."

". . . a giant bowl of twisty noods . . ."

". . . and cosmic cakes!" said Charlotte and Cathy.

The twins had finished each other's sentences for as long as Zack had known them. And he'd known them for his entire life.

When they reached the main floor, Zack moved toward the elevator door. "Last one to the table is a gorblesnoozer!" he yelled.

But the doors stayed closed. Zack stepped back and asked, "Ira, what's going on? Let us out."

The doors suddenly opened as the twins pushed in front and raced to the kitchen first.

"Zack is . . ."

". . . a gorblesnoozer!" they cheered.

"Well then, he must be a starving gorblesnoozer," said Zack's dad.

"I sure am!" Zack said. "And I want breakfast for dinner!"

"That's a great idea," said his dad. "I'll have bacon, eggs, and toast please, Ira."

Four robot arms reached out with plates full of food for the family.

"Master . . . Just . . . Zack . . . ," Ira said slowly. "Here are your cosmic cakes . . . with boingoberry syrup."

Zack stuffed a big piece into his mouth. "Yuck!" He spit the food out.

"My cosmic cakes are covered in *soy sauce*!"

"My galactic patty . . ."

". . . and twisty noods . . ."

". . . aren't even cooked!" added Charlotte and Cathy.

"Oh no, my mistake," said Ira. "I will fix this right away."

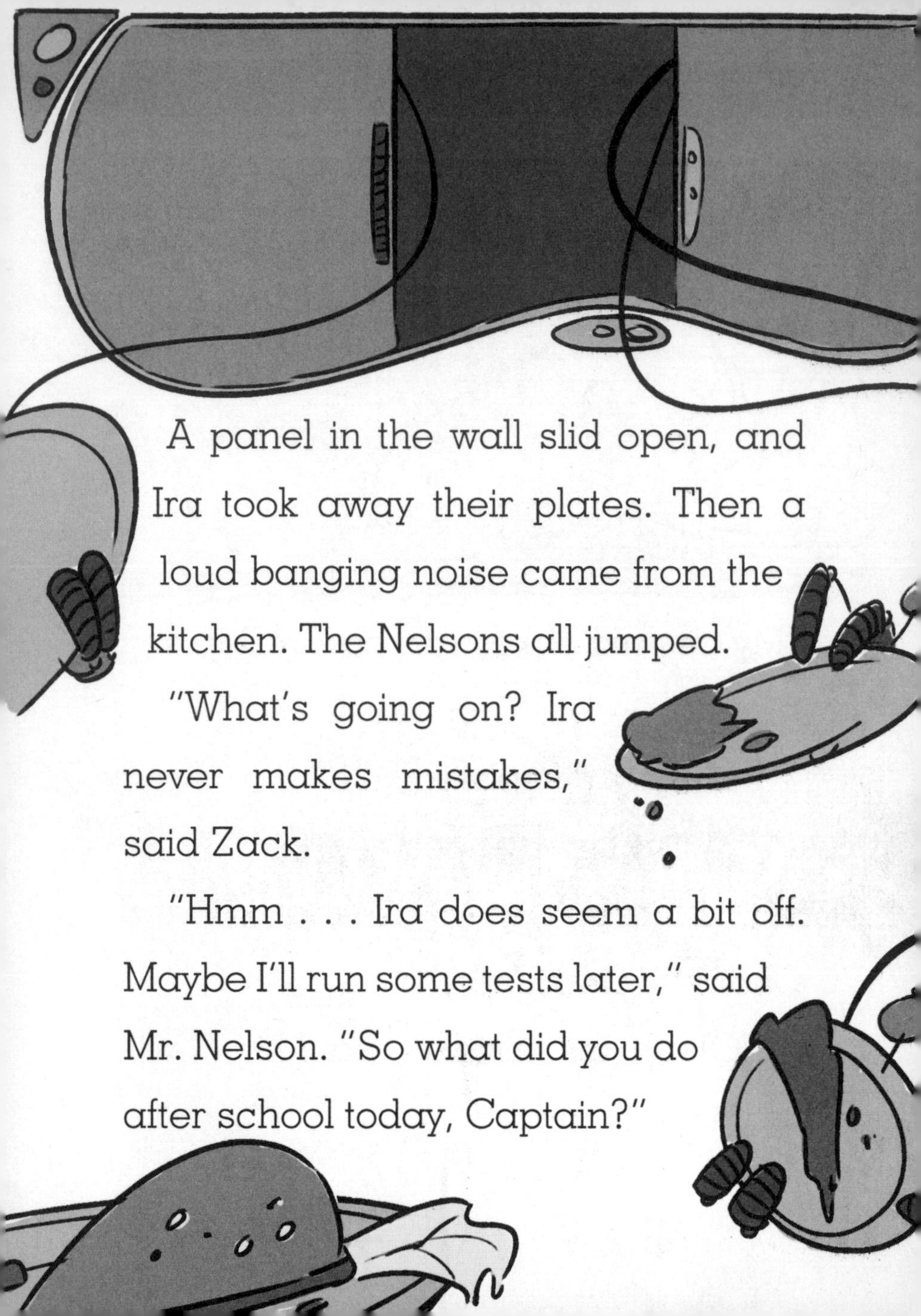

A panel in the wall slid open, and Ira took away their plates. Then a loud banging noise came from the kitchen. The Nelsons all jumped.

"What's going on? Ira never makes mistakes," said Zack.

"Hmm . . . Ira does seem a bit off. Maybe I'll run some tests later," said Mr. Nelson. "So what did you do after school today, Captain?"

Zack smiled. "I played holo-hockey with Drake and Seth at the park."

Holo-hockey was a combination of the Earth sports tennis and hockey. Two teams played in an ice rink with a tennis net in the middle and goals on each end. The players used hockey rackets to

shoot a holo-puck into the other team's goal and score points. It seemed easy, but the holo-hockey rink played against the teams too. Robot holograms could pop up at any time to knock the holo-puck away. It was a super-surprising, super-cool sport, and Zack loved it.

Finally, Ira brought out the food. "I am sorry about the error," the robot said quietly.

Ira set the plates down, and Zack inspected his food. The stack of cosmic cakes was huge, but it tasted great this time.

Zack ate and ate, but there was too much food. "I'm done, Ira. Thanks!"

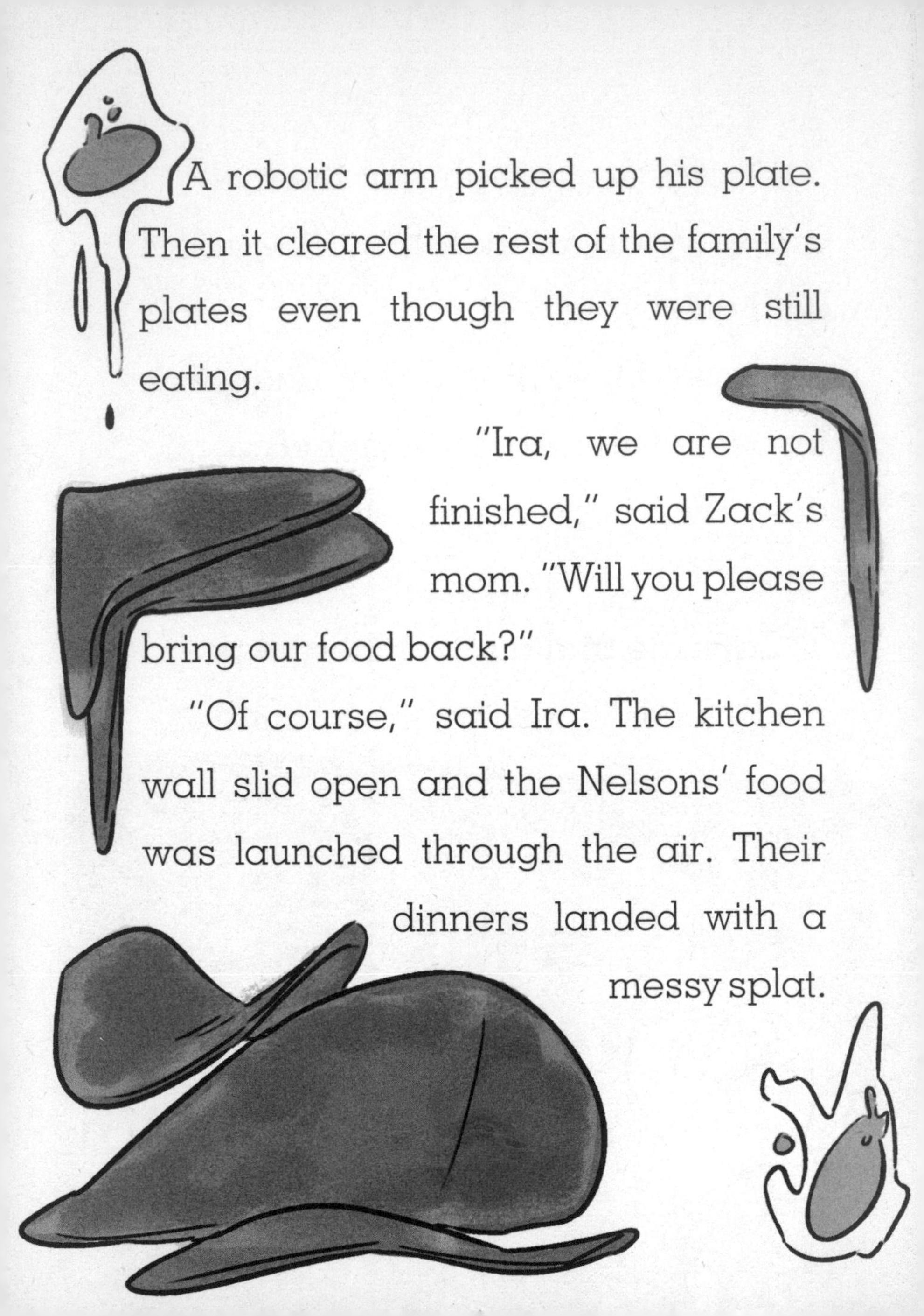

A robotic arm picked up his plate. Then it cleared the rest of the family's plates even though they were still eating.

"Ira, we are not finished," said Zack's mom. "Will you please bring our food back?"

"Of course," said Ira. The kitchen wall slid open and the Nelsons' food was launched through the air. Their dinners landed with a messy splat.

For the first time in his life, Zack's twin sisters were speechless. Their mother held her arms out. She was completely covered in food.

"Well, that was not *egg*-cellent," said their dad as he wiped eggs off his face. "Something is wrong with Ira. I'll run some tests right away. Everything should be okay in the morning."

Chapter 2
Blackout!

When Zack woke up the next morning, his room was pitch-black. *Why is it so dark in here?* Zack wondered.

"Zack, wake up!" a high-pitched voice called out.

He paused for a moment. "Ira? Is that you?"

"No, it's Mom!" Mrs. Nelson looked like she'd just woken up too. "Here's a lantern. Hurry and get dressed for school!"

Zack stumbled in the darkness. He bumped into his desk and accidentally stepped on Luna's tail. Luna let out a sharp cry. "Sorry, Luna! I can't see anything! Ira, can you turn on the lights?"

There was no answer. The entire house was quiet.

Zack got dressed as fast as he could. Then he rushed to the elevator with Luna, but it wasn't working.

At the bottom of the stairs, Zack's dad was looking at an electrical panel. "Morning, Captain. Looks like we lost power."

"Wow," said Zack. "So no lights, no hyperphones, no web-screens—"

"And no IRA," Dad said. "Everything is off."

"Hurry up," his mom said again as she rushed down the stairs with his sisters. "And take these. It's very dark today."

She handed the kids old-fashioned flashlights from Earth. Zack and his sisters turned on their flashlights as Mom shuffled them outside.

All the lights in the neighborhood were off . Only a few dim stars sparkled in the sky.

Following their flashlights, Zack and his sisters walked to the bus stop. Seth and Drake were already there. They were each holding nebu-crystals that lit up the sidewalk.

"It is so dark out, huh?" said Seth nervously as he put his crystal around his neck.

"I bet the power will turn back on any minute," said Zack.

"I do not think so," said Drake. "This is a cosmic blackout."

"A what?" asked Zack.

"It is a type of storm on Nebulon," Drake explained as he pointed to the sky. "It is very rare. The storm clouds drain all the power on the planet and block out the light."

"This is the first cosmic blackout in years," added Seth. He looked around in the darkness. "It will pass like any storm, but it is a little scary."

"So it's like a blizzard on Earth!" said Zack excitedly. "That's when it snows a lot and everyone stays home."

"But we do not," said Drake. "Rain, sleet, blackout, or torgs, school will always be open. We should walk. The speedybus is not coming today."

The kids all started down the street. As they walked through the darkness, Zack noticed that Seth kept looking around. It was almost as if he was looking for something in the shadows.

Chapter 3
School in the Dark

ARR-OOOHHH! A whining noise rang out from a bush near the kids.

Seth quickly hid behind the rest of the group. "Something is following us!" he cried.

Zack pointed his flashlight at the bush. "Hmm . . . I don't see anything."

"But I heard something!" Seth insisted nervously.

"Oh, I am sure there is nothing to be afraid of," said Drake, walking on. "Come on. Let us go inside."

Drake led the way into the school building. The building had lost power, but floating emergency glo-lamps lit up the hallways. Mr. Spudnik, the principal, was ushering students into the auditorium.

Once everyone took their seats, Mr. Spudnik walked onto the stage. "Good morning, Sprockets Academy. As I am sure you already know, we are having a cosmic blackout that has drained all power on Nebulon."

A hush fell over the students as the glo-lamps flickered in the room.

The principal continued. "The storm will pass tomorrow, and all systems will be up and running then. But in the meantime, all classes are canceled!"

"Yippee wah-wah!" all the students cheered.

Seth looked especially happy. Maybe this meant they could all go home. But Seth's face fell as the principal waved for the students to quiet down. "Instead of class, we will have a Cosmic Field Day! All students are welcome to use the school fields and special blackout equipment in the gym. Be careful and have fun!"

As soon as the announcement ended, Zack and Drake rushed to the gym with their crystals. Drake gave Zack a crystal too, while Seth followed slowly behind.

"Do you know what we can play without power?" asked Drake.

"Let's find out!" said Zack as he went into the gym. "Awesome! There are glow-in-the-dark soccer balls, basketballs, and hockey sticks in here! They even have glow-in-the-dark baseball gear!"

With a smile, Zack held up glow-in-the-dark mitts, helmets, and bats. His friends looked confused.

"What in the cosmos are these for?" asked Drake, confused.

Zack smiled. "Get ready to play ball . . . Earth-style!"

Chapter 4
Batter Up!

The friends grabbed the glow-in-the-dark sports gear and headed outside. The field was crowded, but they found a place to play.

"Baseball is like galactic blast, but instead of robots, you throw, catch, and hit the ball yourself!" Zack explained.

Zack handed Seth a glowing baseball glove. "Why don't you try catching
the ball?" Zack said.

Seth put the glove on his head.

"No, you wear the glove on your
hand," Zack said.

"I knew that," said Seth. "I was just testing you."

"Okay," said Zack. Then he walked over to Drake. "Here's the ball."

Drake set the ball on the ground and tried to kick it.

Zack waved his arms. "No! First, hold the ball in your palm. Then, take aim and throw!" Zack pretended to throw the ball.

Drake mimicked Zack's posture and lifted his arm up, but he let go of the ball behind himself. Drake was embarrassed.

"It's okay!" Zack encouraged him. "Try again!"

Drake tried again and again, but the ball kept falling behind him. Zack showed him the steps again. This time Drake lifted his arm over his shoulder and threw the ball as hard as he could. The glowing ball soared high into the air.

"Nice one, Drake!" yelled Zack. "Now catch it, Seth!"

Seth held out his glove and closed his eyes. The ball landed with a clap inside his glove!

"Great catch!" cheered Zack. "Now let's try to play a real game!"

Zack moved the others into position. Drake was the pitcher. Seth was the outfielder. Zack picked up the bat.

"Throw me the ball," he told Drake.

Drake pitched the ball and Zack hit it high into the air.

"Oh no! What now?" cried Seth in a panic.

"You have to catch the ball!" Zack shouted.

The ball flew over Seth and went into the forest by the school. Seth stopped. He wouldn't go into the forest.

"Can you find the ball, Seth?" asked Zack. "It's probably the only thing glowing in the dark forest."

Seth slumped his shoulders. "This game is no fun."

"Oh, never mind!" Zack said as he ran over. "Look! There's the ball."

Zack picked up the ball as Drake joined them.

"Seth is right. This game is hard without robots," Drake said. "Can we play something else?"

Zack thought for moment, and then he smiled. "I know something you will get a *kick* out of."

Chapter 5
Mystery in the Dark

After a quick lunch, the boys had switched their baseball equipment for glow-in-the-dark jerseys and soccer cleats. Then they set up glowing goal nets at each end of the field.

"Soccer is much simpler than baseball," Zack assured his friends.

"All you need is a ball to kick." Zack held up a glow-in-the-dark soccer ball. "This sport is like holo-hockey only there are no robots, no hockey rackets, and no net in the middle of the field. Oh, and players try to kick the ball into the goal, and they can't ever use their hands."

"It already sounds confusing," said Drake jokingly.

Zack smiled and patted Drake on the back. Then he gently passed him the ball with his foot. "Try kicking the ball!"

The glowing net was not far away. Drake drew back his leg and swung it forward. But instead of striking the ball, he kicked up a mound of dirt and fell down.

Zack helped him up. "Try again."

This time Drake kicked the ball. It slowly rolled into the net.

"GOOOOOOOAL!" Zack cheered as he did a little celebratory jig. "Isn't this fun, guys?"

Drake and Seth laughed.

Next, Zack dribbled the ball all the way down the field. His friends tried to keep up, but they were running out of energy. Then Zack kicked the ball to Seth. Seth stopped it with his heel, and

he sped toward the goal. But just as he lifted his leg to make the final kick, he lost his balance and fell down. "It is easier to control an airboard than to kick that moving ball!" exclaimed Seth.

Zack ran over to help him up. "But once you get the hang of it, it's super-fun!"

"More like super-exhausting," Drake said, out of breath. He plopped down on the ground and fell backward. "All this running is making me hungry. We only had one choice for lunch . . . and only one serving."

Seth nodded in agreement.

Zack looked down disappointedly. After a long pause, he had a new idea. "Why don't we go eat at my house after school?" he suggested.

"Sounds delicious!" Seth said. Drake nodded in agreement and sat up.

Just then a strange noise echoed across the field. *ARR-OOOHHHH!*

"There it is again!" Seth shouted. "Did you hear that?"

"Hear what?" Zack asked. "Don't worry. I'm sure it's nothing."

Zack pointed his flashlight into the forest to show him. Sure enough, there was nothing to see but trees.

Then Seth's stomach growled so loud that everyone could hear it.

"It might just be your stomach," Zack teased. "Come on. Let's clean up before the bell rings!"

Chapter 6
Hidden Pantry

Back at the house, Luna excitedly welcomed Zack and his friends home. The power was still out—except for a few floating orb candles that gave off a soft glow. They hovered in the air along the walls.

Mr. Nelson was out on the patio.

Smoke poured out of the barbecue grill.

"Wowzers! How is there smoke coming from the grill?" asked Drake.

"Well, since the solar cubes aren't working, I used an old-fashioned tool as fuel—wood!" explained Mr. Nelson.

He tossed more wood into the fire. "Now, who wants to make pizza?"

"We do!" shouted the boys.

"Well then, into the kitchen!" said Zack's dad.

The boys rushed inside. Charlotte and Cathy were sitting at the table with their mom.

"I have always wondered what's inside Ira's kitchen," said Zack.

Seth and Drake nodded excitedly as Zack's sisters sang together,

"I bet it's filled with . . ."

". . . all kinds of food!"

"Oh, you have no idea," Mrs. Nelson said with a smile. "Watch this." She went to the electrical panel in the hallway and pulled down an emergency latch. Then she pushed on the wall and a hidden room appeared. "Welcome to Ira's hidden pantry," she said.

Zack stepped inside with his flash-light. Then his sisters, Drake, Seth, and Luna followed.

"This is amazing!" said Zack.

There were rows and rows of shelves that went from the floor all the way to the ceiling. The top few stored cold foods like meats, fruits, and vegetables. Next, the middle section stored all of the freezer items like ice cream, ice swirlies, and ready-made galactic patties. Then, the bottom rows stored all the dry foods like Zack's favorite cosmic cake mix, cookies, and jars of Luna's favorite treats.

The kids looked around with their mouths wide open.

"Look up!" Drake called out. He held his nebu-crystal above his head.

Just below the ceiling, a conveyer belt ran across the entire room. Hanging from the top of the ceiling was a pair of large mechanical claws.

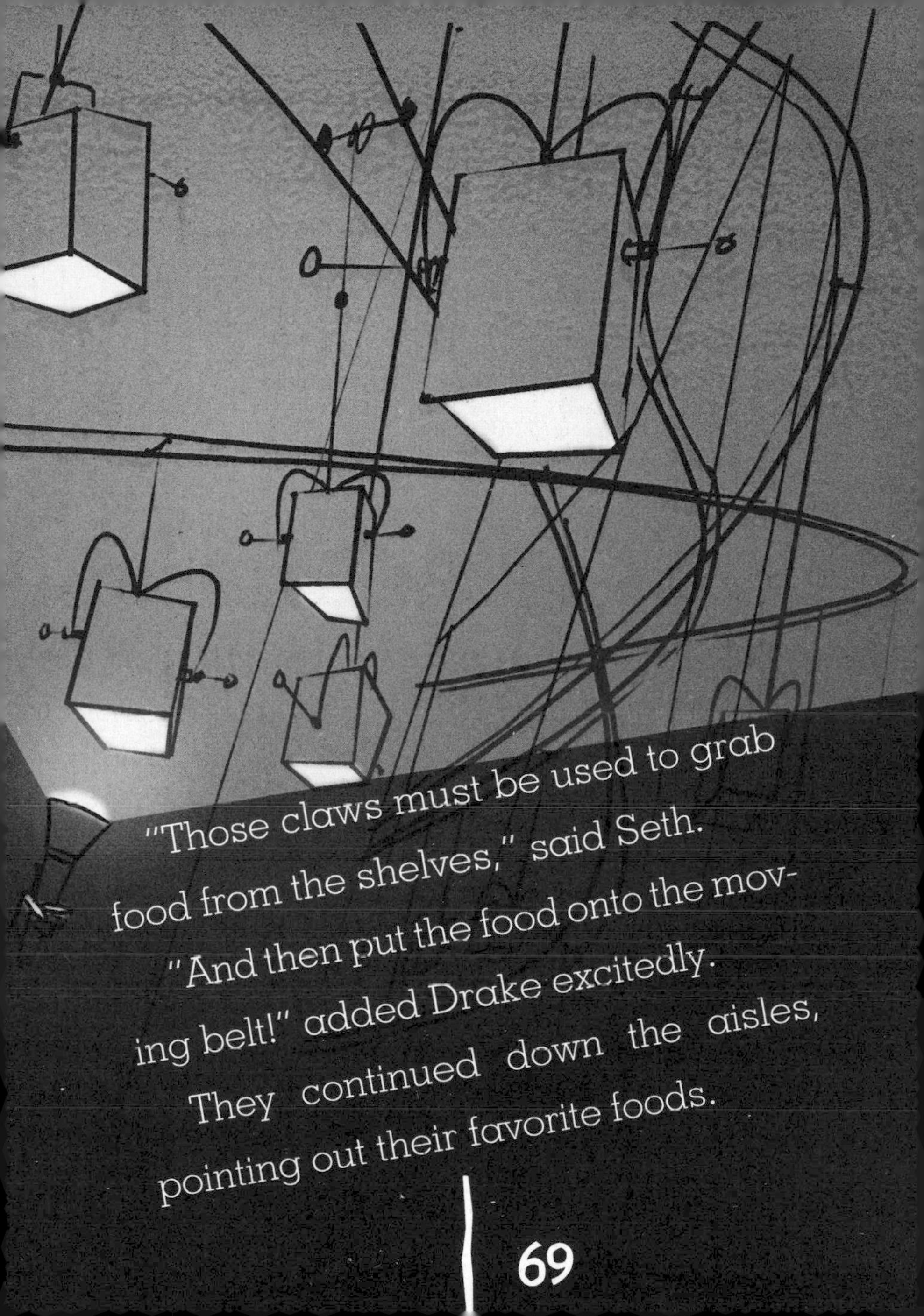

"Those claws must be used to grab food from the shelves," said Seth.

"And then put the food onto the moving belt!" added Drake excitedly.

They continued down the aisles, pointing out their favorite foods.

Soon, they came to another door. Zack stepped inside first. This hidden room had all of the appliances. Stovetop burners and ovens lined the wall. A set of chopping blades and six gigantic mixers were on the counter, but since the power was out, nothing was turned on.

"Wow. No wonder Ira can make our food so fast," said Drake as his stomach made a loud growling noise.

"So what are we waiting for? Let's get cooking!" exclaimed Zack.

Chapter 7

Pizza Time!

Back in the dining room, Mrs. Nelson handed each kid an apron. "These pizzas won't make themselves! It's time to get messy!"

Zack and his friends eagerly helped one another put on their aprons.

How hard could it be to cook pizzas?

Zack thought. *After all, Ira makes it super-fast.*

Once everyone was settled, Zack's mom started giving directions. First, she handed Seth a jar of pizza sauce.

"Here, open this." Seth took the jar and tried to twist the lid off, but it wouldn't budge.

"Ugh . . . I cannot get it open," said Seth breathlessly.

"Then try tapping the lid on the counter," said Mrs. Nelson.

Seth turned the jar upside down. After a few firm taps, he heard the lid pop. Seth then turned the jar right side up and tried it again. This time it easily twisted open.

Drake helped the twins wash and prepare the vegetables.

Zack worked on the dough. He threw in all the ingredients and started mixing as fast as he could. "Gosh, this is harder than it looks," he said as he wiped his cheek. His whole face was covered in flour.

"Here, let me try," said Seth.

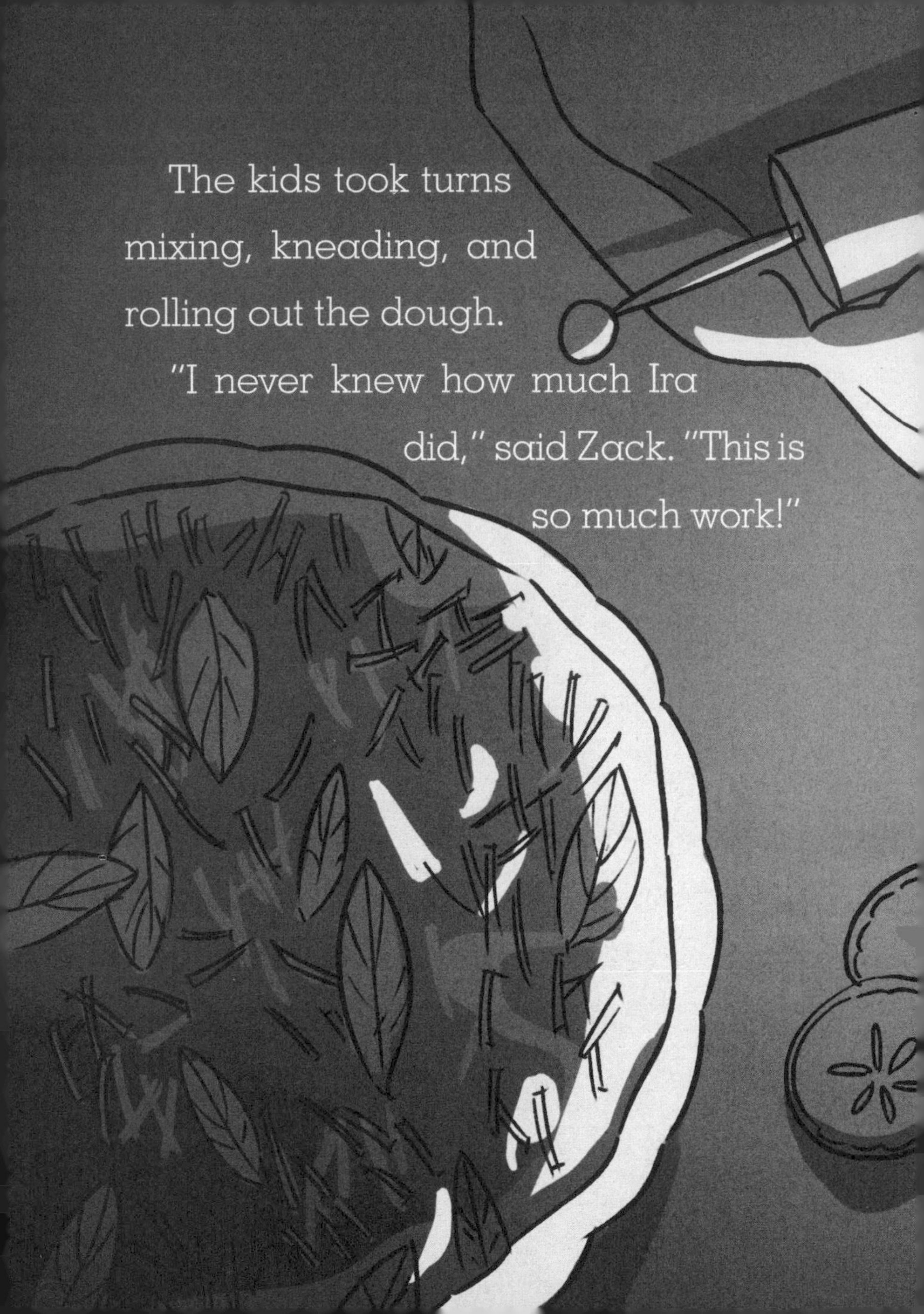

The kids took turns mixing, kneading, and rolling out the dough.

"I never knew how much Ira did," said Zack. "This is so much work!"

"Tell me about it!" Seth exclaimed as he took a deep breath.

After adding all the toppings, the pizza was ready for the grill. Zack's dad placed the pizza onto the fire. A little while later, it was finally time to eat.

"Wow, that looks so yumzers!" said Seth. The cheese was bubbling and sizzling on top.

The boys were about to dig in when Zack paused. "Hold on. Where are the plates? And we have no napkins or glasses for our spudsy melonade."

"Well, Ira always sets the table," said Zack's mom. "Without him, you'll have to set it yourselves."

"Oh right. . . . Ira really did do everything for us," Zack replied.

Zack walked to the kitchen. After opening every single drawer, he finally found the utensils and cups. He carried as much as he could back to the table.

The others helped set the table while Zack's mom cut the pizza into slices. Then Zack served his friends.

Drake took a bite and his eyes closed with joy. "Wow, this pizza is amazing!"

Zack agreed, but he couldn't say a word. His mouth was full of food.

Chapter 8
Seth Faces His Fears

Before they knew it, all the pizza had disappeared. The boys were stuffed!

Zack finished his last bite and slumped under the table. "That was great! Hey, Mom, do we still have that glow-pro basketball somewhere in the garage? We can set up a hoop in the

backyard to play basketball before it gets dark."

Drake laughed. "Zack, it has been dark all day!"

"Oh yeah," said Zack. "I forgot that this wasn't a normal day."

"We do still have the glow-pro ball," his mom said. Then she motioned to the dirty plates on the table. "But you're not going anywhere until after you clean up."

"Clean up?" asked Zack. "Oh right. Ira's not here to do it. . . ." His voice trailed off. "Okay, guys. Looks like we're on cleanup duty."

Zack and his friends carefully stacked the dishes and carried them to the sink while his sisters helped their dad clean the grill.

"Why don't you all choose one task and help one another?" suggested Mrs. Nelson.

"I'll wash the dishes," said Zack.

"And I will dry them," said Drake. He grabbed a dish towel.

"Then I will put the dishes away," said Seth.

Thirty minutes later, suds were everywhere and the boys were still washing and cleaning up.

"I never knew doing dishes took so long," Drake said as he wiped down the last plate. "Ira does them all in no time!"

"Once Ira's back I have to thank him for everything he does," agreed Zack.

After doing the dishes, the kids had to clean up the mess they had made in the kitchen. The boys scrubbed the counters while the twins organized the cabinets.

An hour later, the kitchen was sparkling clean.

Zack grabbed his flashlight. "Finally, let's go play some basketball!"

Drake and Seth looked tired as they followed him outside.

"Zack, I do not think we have energy to play another Earth sport," said Drake. "Just look at Seth."

Seth was slumped on the ground near Zack's back door. Suddenly, a mysterious sound echoed in the distance.

ARR-OOOHHH!

Seth sat up. "There is the noise again! Did you hear it?"

His friends nodded. Everyone heard it this time.

"It came from that tree," said Zack. He aimed his flashlight into the dark branches. The leaves shook as another cry erupted.

Drake slowly approached the tree and shook the branches. A shadow popped out and darted down the street.

"See?!" cried Seth. "I told you something was following us!"

"You're right. Let's follow it!" said Zack.

The boys chased the shadow

through their neighborhood until it disappeared into a bush.

Drake slowly crept up from behind. "I see it inside," he whispered.

Then a pair of glowing eyes peered back at the kids through the bushes. Seth started to back away, but it was too late. The creature leaped out of the bushes.

Chapter 9
A New Pet

A furry animal landed right in Seth's arms! He lifted the critter, holding it gently with both hands. It looked like a puppy mixed with a butterfly. Soft brown fur covered its sweet puppy face, but its ears were like brightly colored yellow and red butterfly wings.

"You are so cute!" said Seth as he petted the animal. It nuzzled Seth back. "I cannot believe I was scared of such an adorable little creature!"

"ARR-OOOHHH!" the animal said in agreement. It made the noise again as its ears began to glow in the dark.

"That's what looked like glowing eyes," said Zack. "I wonder what other tricks this little guy can do."

As if to answer Zack's question, the animal's ears started to flap up and down. Swiftly, it fluttered high up into the air.

"Wow! It can fly!" cheered Drake.

The creature left a trail of light in the dark sky. It was unlike anything Zack had ever seen.

"Do you know what this animal is?" asked Zack.

"I have no idea," said Seth as the animal landed on his shoulder and licked his face.

Drake laughed. "Well, I think you have made a new friend, Seth."

"I think you are right, Drake," said Seth, smiling. "I am going to ask my parents if I can keep him!"

The animal flew up into the air again. Zack and his friends looked up to watch it streak across the night. Then stars began to glow.

"Hey, look! Stars!" Zack exclaimed. "I think the cosmic blackout is ending!"

"Oh." Drake sounded sad. "I had a fun time doing things ourselves. Making pizzas, playing baseball . . . maybe we can do it again sometime?"

"Yeah, it has been a pretty grape day," Seth agreed. "Minus doing the dishes." The friends all laughed.

"But next time, let's play those Earth sports in the daylight," said Zack with a grin. "I promise, they're completely different when you can see everything."

Seth's new friend fluttered back down and landed in Seth's arms. "Do you want to go for a walk, little guy?" asked Seth.

The creature flapped its ears happily and followed Seth down the street. Zack and Drake followed behind.

As they walked on, the creature once again flew into the air as its ears glowed brightly. This time, it yipped with excitement.

A new buzzing sound rattled above them and the boys looked at one another. What could this new noise mean? Then the entire street bright-ened as the streetlights all clicked back on. The moons shined brightly and stars sparkled in the sky.

"The power is back!" said Zack.

"Yippee wah-wah!" Seth and Drake cheered.

"But now it's really nighttime," said Seth with a laugh.

So the boys said good-bye and went their separate ways. Except for Seth's new friend, who followed Seth all the way home.

Chapter 10

Do It Yourself

The next morning Zack woke up as Luna licked his face. It was pitch-black, just like the day before. He immediately jumped out of bed.

"Master Just Zack! Is everything okay? Let me turn on the lights." It was Ira's voice.

"Ira! You're back!" Zack exclaimed excitedly. "I missed you so much!" Luna yipped with excitement too.

"Thank you, Master Just Zack," replied Ira. "It is good to be back. Would you like me to start the tooth-o-matic cleaner-flosser for you?"

"No, that's okay, Ira. I can brush my own teeth," said Zack as he walked into the bathroom.

After getting dressed, Zack went out to the hallway but paused at the elevator. "Hey, Luna, let's take the stairs."

"Excuse me? Master Just Zack, but the elevator would be faster," Ira began.

But Zack and Luna were already on their way down. "I know, but a walk to breakfast sounds nice."

His mom, dad, and sisters were already at the table.

"Goodness," said Ira. "Everyone is ahead of schedule today. Would you like some cosmic cakes with boingoberry syrup, Master Just Zack?"

"That sounds great," said Zack. "Ira, I didn't realize how much you do until this cosmic blackout. Thanks for helping with everything."

"You are welcome, Master Just Zack," Ira replied. "I am happy to be back."

"Although I actually kind of liked doing things for myself," continued Zack. "It was like being back on Earth."

"Oh? Then would you like to make the cosmic cakes and clean up, too?" asked Ira.

Zack laughed. "Well, since you had a day off, I'm sure you missed cooking, right? Though maybe you could teach me some of your recipes?"

Ira agreed, then he quickly whipped up the food.

After breakfast, Zack met his friends at the bus stop. Seth's new pet was perched on his shoulder.

"Guess what?" asked Seth. "My parents said I can keep him! We are going to go to the vet after school. And

since we found him during the cosmic blackout, I decided to call him Cosmo!"

"Grape name!" said Zack.

"He has to come to school with me because he refuses to leave my side," Seth explained.

Zack smiled as he watched Seth and his new pet. Just yesterday, Seth had been so afraid of the dark, but without the blackout, he may have never found Cosmo. Life was funny like that on Nebulon.

That morning before class, kids were sharing what they did during the blackout when Mrs. Rudolph walked in.

Mrs. Rudolph noticed Seth's odd-looking creature immediately. "Wow, Seth! You have a noctis! Where did you find him?"

"A noctis! So that is what he is called!" Seth nuzzled Cosmo again. "It is a funny thing, because, well, Cosmo kind of found me."

"That's amazing," Mrs. Rudolph said. "Noctis rarely ever show themselves because they live in the dark, unless they find the right friend. Oh, there's so much to learn about the noctis."

Suddenly, Zack had the perfect idea. He shot his hand in the air. "Mrs. Rudolph, can we learn more about the noctis outside?"

"Oh, what a great idea, Zack!" his teacher said. "I think we've all earned a day in the sun."

"Awesome!" the students called out.

Cosmo flew excitedly into the air and led the class outside. Zack put his arms around Drake and Seth. Nebulon had some amazing inventions. After all, he loved playing games on his vid-screen. But after the blackout, Zack realized that he didn't need fancy gadgets to have a good time. All he needed were his friends.